This

 bang on the door™©

book belongs to

_____

_____

_____

_____

_____

bee

elephant

rabbit

kangaroo

bear

squid

hippo

plankton

zebra

bug

whale

pea brain

worm

penguin

horse

brain
cell

jellyfish sheep

rat

crab

amoeba

aardvark

cat

bat

polar bear

hedgehog

shark

slug

pig

puffin

moose

dolphin

dog

snail

duck billed platypus

spider

armadillo

To marc and JJ
with love, Mum
JR

First published in 1997 by
David Bennett Books Limited
United Kingdom.

First paperback edition published 1999.

BRITISH LIBRARY CATALOGUING IN PUBLICATION DATA
A catalogue record for this book is available from the British Library.

ISBN 1-85602-319-2

Production by Imago
Printed in Singapore

The story of
brain cell

Created by bang on the door™

Illustrated by
Karen Duncan and Samantha Stringle

Story by
Jackie Robb and Berny Stringle

David Bennett Books

Brain Cell was so brainy
he talked in riddles and rhyme.

confused people!

when people tried to
solve them
it took up lots of time.

If a door is ajar
can a jar be a door?

Do waves wave goodbye
when they leave the seashore?

Can you tie a rainbow?

Or see a moonbeam?

Can you eat jellyfish?

Or hear ice cream?

Do snowmen dress up
to dance at snowballs?

Will the pleasure boat trip when the waterfalls?

will the bread run out,

when the butterflies?

Can you see the sunflower?

Or eat magpies?

Does a dogfish?

Does a cowslip?

Can a horsefly?

Brain Cell told them all
each person and creature,

They could learn these things
if he was their teacher.

Bat said, "Fantastic!"
Bug said, "Oh great!"

Aardvark and Zebra said,
"You've got a date."

So they sat in his classroom and all called him 'Prof',

And he talked and he talked
'til they all nodded off.

bee

elephant

rabbit

kangaroo

bear

hippo

squid

plankton

zebra

bug

whale

pea brain

worm

horse

brain cell

penguin

jellyfish

sheep

rat

crab

amoeba

aardvark

cat

bat

polar bear

hedgehog

shark

slug

pig

puffin

moose

dolphin

dog

snail

duck billed platypus

spider

armadillo